Barn

Written and Illustrated by DEBBY ATWELL

HOUGHTON MIFFLIN COMPANY 🦃 BOSTON 1996

Walter Lorraine *wl* Books

Library of Congress Cataloging-in-Publication Data

Atwell, Debby.
 Barn / Debby Atwell.
  p. cm.
  Summary: Follows the life of a country barn from the late
eighteenth-century to the present day.
  ISBN 0-395-78568-5
  [1. Barns—Fiction.] I. Title
PZ7.B8935Bar 1996
[E]—dc20   96-11044
                                                                      CIP
                                                                       AC

For information about this and other Houghton Mifflin trade and
reference books and multimedia products, visit The Bookstore at
Houghton Mifflin on the World Wide Web at
http://www.hmco.com/trade/.

Printed in the United States of America

HOR   10   9   8   7   6   5   4   3   2   1

For

CARRIE SHERMAN

I was raised in a coastal fog so thick the crows had to walk to the cornfield that morning. Indians called the land *Winnacunnett,* which means, "The pine trees are having a good laugh." The settlers called the place Hampton, after a town in England. It took twenty men sawing, fitting, and lifting beams, and a flock of womenfolk cooking food to raise me that day. They sang songs about winning the Revolution.

For over a hundred years I was a plain old farm barn. In my early days, Ben would come in before every sunup to feed the cows, horses, pigs, and goats.

Then, he'd take them to pasture and I'd stand quiet all day, with an east wind off the Atlantic blowing through my two big doors. Life was all around me: babies growing, corn ripening, leaves turning, snow falling.

Ben's son, Ezra, loved horses. In the winter, Ezra just about lived in a one-horse open sleigh. That boy even made up a song about the harness bells jingling. Had a catchy little tune to it. *Jingle, jingle...bells, bells.* I can't quite remember that tune, but I'll never forget Ezra and his horses.

Ezra's daughter, Viola, ran the farm when he got old. Then Zeke, Viola's son, took over. One day, a man from town told Zeke he'd have to go. He owed the bank too much money.

Zeke left and the Great Depression arrived. The whole country was out of work. Homeless men—they called them hoboes—camped out here.

Polly bought the farm in an auction. Her boys built an addition to the house to make it an inn for people who vacationed at the beach.

When that was done, they cleaned me up. But instead of getting animals, they hauled in all sorts of fancy-looking things called antiques. Polly hammered up a sign, and people came by and bought things.

BUILT BY REUBEN LAMPREY

The boys grew up, got married, and moved away. Then World War II broke out and they went to fight. Their wives and children came to live with Polly.

President Roosevelt asked the whole country to plant victory gardens and gather up metal to make warplanes. Some neighborhood kids hitched up their pony wagon and went around collecting things made of metal. I stored that scrap for them until the government truck came to pick it up.

When the war was won, the boys came home. After they got tired of hugging, kissing, and cooking big meals, Polly's children found new homes and said goodbye. I was wired with electricity because Polly wanted a modern antique shop.

There were many family reunions over the years.

Polly grew old and closed her business. That same year, her granddaughter asked if she could have a small peace rally in me.

The people who came sang songs about peace and love. They were against the war in Vietnam.

A long time later Polly drove up in a taxi. She patted me on the door and said goodbye. I stood silent for many summers.

One spring morning, my new owners, Jack and Lyn, opened my door. They knew a lot about me, but they did not know a lot about squirrels and old electrical wires. Too bad. The squirrels had chewed on the wires to make a nest. Jack turned on the lights and forgot to turn them off. And there I was, on fire. Nothing could stop it. I burned to the ground.

Folks tried to guess how the fire got started. Just about everybody thought it had something to do with the electrical wires and squirrels. I guess the squirrels had more of a reputation than I gave them credit for.

The last thing I recall before a big snow buried what was left of me was seeing Jill, Jack's daughter, heading out to the clothesline.

Winter melted into spring. A bunch of trucks and bulldozers showed up. Carpenters came. The next thing you know, they started to rebuild me just exactly the way I was before the fire. It took about three months to raise me this time. Every Friday, Jack had a big pizza party for the workers.

Hard to believe: there I was, just the same as I was before. But I knew times had changed. I could not help but wonder, *What good is a barn in the modern world?* Anyone could see that farming days were over.

Jack and Lyn worked hard outside all summer. They put in fences and cleared a lot of land. I watched and waited.

In the fall, Jack and Lyn brought me a dozen horses. With this new job, I got back the feeling of being a true barn. It was a good time.

Every morning before sunup, Jack and his kids put the horses out to pasture. I stand quiet all day with an east wind off the Atlantic blowing through my two big doors. And sometimes, I swear, I can hear the pine trees having a good laugh, just like the Indians said. It is some lovely.